Priscilla

AND THE SPLISH-SPLASH SURPRISE

by Nathaniel Hobbie ✶ illustrated by Jocelyn Hobbie

LITTLE, BROWN AND COMPANY

New York ✶ Boston

To Brett

Text copyright © 2006 by Nathaniel Hobbie
Illustrations copyright © 2006 by Jocelyn Hobbie

First Edition: February 2006

Little, Brown and Company

Time Warner Book Group
1271 Avenue of the Americas, New York, NY 10020
Visit our Web site at www.lb-kids.com

Library of Congress Cataloging-in-Publication Data

Hobbie, Nathaniel.
 Priscilla and the splish-splash surprise / by Nathaniel Hobbie ; illustrated by Jocelyn Hobbie.— 1st ed.
   p. cm.
 Summary: Bored after three days of non-stop rain, Priscilla goes outside to perform a rain-stopping dance and meets Posy the Pixie, who shows her the magical land of Primrose and teaches her to appreciate both rain and sunshine.
 ISBN 0-316-01046-4
 [1. Rain and rainfall—Fiction. 2. Boredom—Fiction. 3. Pixies—Fiction. 4. Stories in rhyme.] I. Hobbie, Jocelyn, ill. II. Title.
PZ8.3.H655Pri 2005
[E]—dc22   2004018624

TWP

Printed in Singapore

As we all know, the sky above us is blue.
    But wait just a minute. That's not *always* true.
Sometimes I've noticed, I'm sure you have too,
    the sky turns a purple, green-brownish gray hue.
And that's just how things were looking today
    on that planet of Priscilla's not so far away.

For Priscilla, in fact, there'd been no blue for days.
It started last week with a yellowish haze.
Each day the sky darkened. It thickened like soup.
Finally, the whole sky just seemed to droop.

The first raindrop fell.

Then the second
and third.

Then the clouds opened up and rain was the word.

It came down in buckets. It came down in sheets.
Rain flowed like rivers through backyards and streets.

The fish thought it grand and the frogs sang with glee
and the ducks' kooky quacking seemed quite to agree.

Well, Priscilla is neither a fish nor a duck.
    By her way of thinking, this rain was bad luck.
But bad luck aside, Priscilla's no poop.
    She belongs to the do-what-you-gotta-do group.

She passed a few hours reading in bed.

Did somersaults, back bends, and stood on her head.

She made up a language to teach to her doll.
   But Sally couldn't learn—her brain was too small!
Instead they had tea, but the water got cold.
   The crumpets were crusty; the jam had a mold.

Now this one may stretch the bounds of belief,
 but Priscilla thought *chores* might bring some relief.

So she watered the plants and fed her pet fishes.
 She swept out the dust balls and did all the dishes.
She fluffed up the pillows . . . then flopped to the floor.
 "Oh, bonkers," she cried. "This rain is a bore!"

It rained all that day
    and the day after that.

It kept coming hard. This was no pitter-pat.

By the third day, Priscilla was in quite a stew.

Spinning in circles. Cabin fever beaucoup!

"Egads," she groaned, grabbing fistfuls of hair.
"All this rotten rain is really no fair.
One day of rain, one day would be fine.
But *three* days," she fumed, "is way out of line!"

Sometimes a problem can seem overly large.
But you know Priscilla. She likes to take charge.

"I've got it!" she cried. "I know just what we need.
A rain-*stopping* dance is the way to proceed."

In five minutes flat, perhaps even quicker,
   Priscilla pulled on her rain boots and slicker.
Then, in just one, maybe two minutes more,
   that girl was careening headlong out the door.

splish-

The rain, it was thrashing like waves on the sea.

But did that stop Priscilla? Not her, no siree!

In fact, if you saw how she stomped, splashed, and spun,

you might have supposed she was having some fun.

SPLASH!

Then all of a sudden she stopped, still as stone.
It's that funny feeling, *I'm not alone.*
At the edge of the yard, something did stir.
A pair of eyes flashed. They were looking at her!

Trying hard to ignore her wobbling knees,
    she whispered, "Who's there? Answer me, please."
A voice called out from the edge of the wood,
    "Just having a look. Your dance is quite good."

Hmm, thought Priscilla, *I shouldn't feel scared.*
So she crept toward the woods as close as she dared.
"Who are you?" she asked. "I wish I could see.
Perhaps we could even be friends, you and me."

"Friends?" the voice giggled. "Friends, yes indeed.
I like your rain dance. So we're friends, it's agreed!"
And then, through the leaves, a pink face peeked out.

"Ohh," gasped Priscilla. "You're a *pixie*, no doubt."

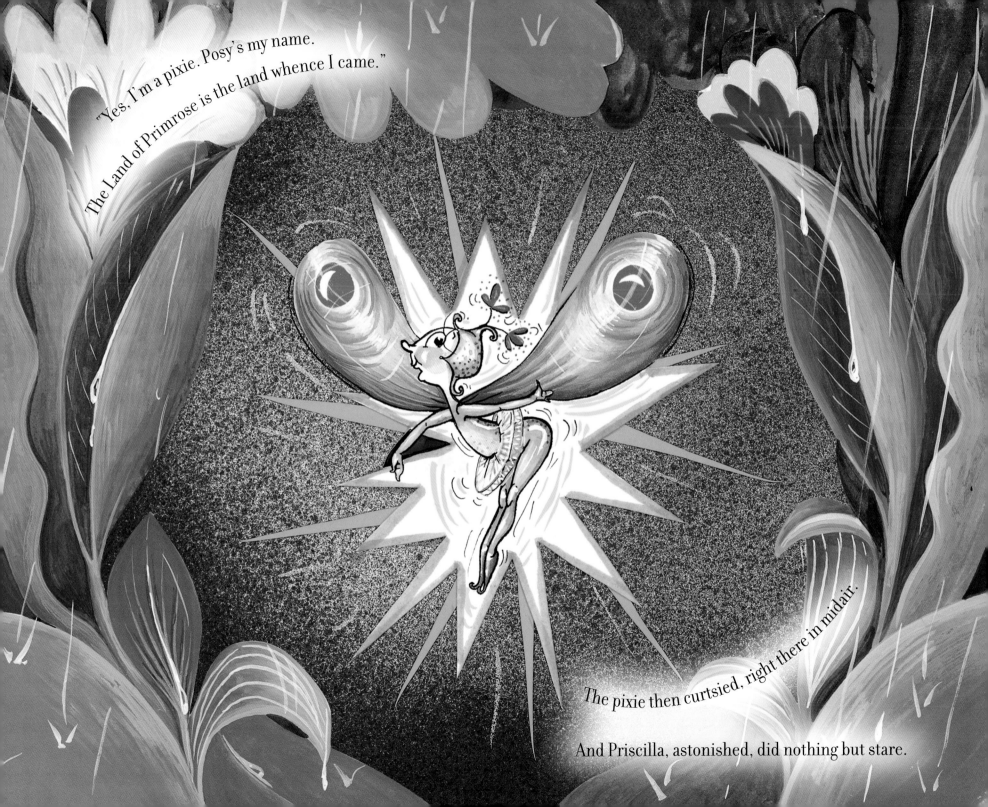

"Yes, I'm a pixie. Posy's my name.
The Land of Primrose is the land whence I came."

The pixie then curtsied, right there in midair.

And Priscilla, astonished, did nothing but stare.

"You're funny," laughed Posy, in a perfect plié.

"I mean that, of course, in a wonderful way.

When storm clouds roll in, most people complain.

I'm glad to see someone enjoying the rain!"

Well, Priscilla was trying to gather her wits.
   "But, Posy," she pleaded, "this rain is the pits.
I didn't come out to have fun, not a chance!
   I came out to do a rain-stopping dance."

"My, my," replied Posy, full of concern.
"I see you still have a few things to learn."

Then Posy, that pixie, swooped back to the wood.

"Wait!" cried Priscilla, cinching her hood.

"I'm sorry," she called. "I don't mean to be rude."

"Come back. *PLEASE* come back, little pixie," she wooed.

Priscilla scrunched up her face and stared at her shoe.
Then it was clear, there was only one thing to do. . . .

The forest was glowing a radiant green.
Every plant glistened with a sparkling sheen.

Raindrops were clinging to leaflets like jewels,
and all was reflected in shimmering pools.

Then, once again, that pixie appeared.

Whirling and twirling, "Oh, goody!" she cheered.

"I knew you were special. Just follow me.

There are so many things I want you to see."

"Look here," Posy called. "The Funk Funnel Vine.
The smell isn't great but its funneling's divine.

And the Bob-Along Beetle.

The Umbrella Flower.

The Muck Mover Mole
has come out for his shower!"

"Just get a gander at the Great Gargling Crane.
    All of these creatures, they live for the rain!"

"Yes," laughed Priscilla, "I can see that it's true.
They all look so happy, I'm feeling it too."

"The rain used to seem such a dreary old bore.
I understand now it's about so much more!"

"There are worlds within worlds. An endless array.
Look closer, and you'll see things a new way."

To Priscilla it seemed something new had begun.
Then the clouds opened up and out burst the sun.